My Rhymes Have Reasons

Written by: Chos3nOn3Sp3aks

Cover Illustrated by: Metroxix3c

TABLE OF CONTENTS

Foreword

This manuscript is a poetry book of real-life situations. I wrote and added various pieces with all different stories and situations I am hoping that what's inside of this book will have some answers or information that can help someone's life. It is not just about one topic, but I still recommend you be at least 18 years or older to read this book. These pieces cover a variety of topics, tell little stories of love, hate, deceit, friendship, vulnerability, death, family, love, sex, betrayal anger, abuse, overcoming, strength, fantasy violence happiness, peace, and many other topics of real-life things we as people run across from day to day living. This poetry is for the grown minded adults as I do not filter my work. I say it the way I feel it raw and unapologetic. That is what my readers want and will get. Most people understand life, love, the pursuit of happiness, and have been through things in life, both good and bad. I wrote these pieces from my life experiences, and the experiences of people I know. I also wrote some of these pieces as requests for other people's situations. Also, some are written from my imagination more of a what if or a passing thought scenario. I write for happy and sad occasions. Life has inspired me to write these rhymes for different reasons. It is soothing for my soul to write pieces that are soothing for your soul. Something eclectic to read. I am now grateful for the experiences I have had in my life, positive and negative. Without those experiences I wouldn't have anything to write about.

Warning: This title contains graphic language, descriptions of abuse and violence, very explicit descriptions of sexual encounters or episodes, and a very vivid imagery of an erotic nature. This is a work of fiction. Names, characters, businesses, places, events, brands, media, and incidents are either the products of the author's imagination or used in a fictitious manner. The author acknowledges the trademarked status and trademark owners of various products referenced in this work of fiction, which have been used without permission. The publication or use of these trademarks is not authorized, associated with, or sponsored by the trademark owners. Any resemblance to actual persons or actual events is purely coincidental. All characters in these writings or stories are over 18 years of age, and all sexual activity is safe, freaky and consensual by all of the parties involved. Thank you for your support. Please leave an honest review of this book? It would mean a lot to me and help others to read it. Thanks in advance.

Dedications

I dedicate this book to my children Darius Davon, Denzel Raheim, Diamond Lynn-Marquis, and Destiny Aaliyah. I also want to dedicate this book to my four hype grandchildren. As of the publication date of this book I have four Sugar-lumps (They call me Sugar). Saige Payton, Cohen Cole, Wynter Shai, and my little bow-legged princess Camille Elise. I love all of them and I am striving for greatness for all of them

 I can't forget to shout out my mother Gustavia and my father Adam who has been a great dad to me although I was a young adult when they got married, we have bonded over the years as if I'm his biologically. They may not read my work, for religious reasons, but they are very supportive and proud of me.

Special shoutout to my talented nephew Landon for doing the cover for this book. Please hit him up on IG:metroxix3c. To my old Mocospace writing crew from back in the day I did it again please read and support with reviews like we used to do before social media was actually popping...lol Hey PBD I know you are going to check it out!

Also shout out to my sister Vanessa she is always showing support and sending encouraging words for everything I decide to try to accomplish in my life. I need the support and I appreciate the love.

I have read more than a few poetry books in my life and I haven't seen any that summarize the purpose of the poems, before reading the poem so having discussed the concept with Richard, (hubby) the man of my dreams. I started gathering some my favorite written pieces that would tell a story. It is a dream for me to write this book. It is one of a kind and I hope that it will be successful at getting readers what they need. I hope you enjoy this book finished with summaries. poems and all. I hope my words can offer you growth, and peace through all of life's journeys, because it includes something for everyone regardless of race, age, nationality, or gender. I know that this gift and love of writing is owed all to God. For that I am thankful. Nothing, nothing, nothing can be done without God. Thank you all for choosing this book and I hope you enjoy reading it I am Chos3nOn3Sp3aks and>> **"My Rhymes Have Reasons."**

Summary**This is the first piece written for the title of this book. It tells you about my rhymes and how they heal, relieve, and offer a little of that I can relate to your life. I want my work to enhance your thoughts, relax you into your Calgon, or exhale moments. I want to invoke honest thoughts when you read my pieces. I want conversations to be had. I want feelings of joy or pain evoked. I want these pieces to inspire you to reach for the stars, claim your dreams, and feel the love, anger, or peace I write about. I want you to finish a piece and think gurrrrl get out of my head. I want you to wish I was there speaking to you so you could high five me when you are done reading. I want you to laugh, cry, get mad and smile. Most of all I want you to enjoy the pieces, because all of my rhymes have reasons.

My Rhymes Have Reasons

My rhymes have many reasons, written
for a specific, time place or reason*
My rhymes are for first days or last days*
My rhymes cover flirt days or church days*
Tears or tears of joy for whatever time, place or season*
I just write it down, hoping people read it*
Never knowing the pain I'll be easing*

I just know that when I write most times it's self-relieving*
My rhymes are not for teasing*
Maybe just a little pleasing*
Let your body be free, the day is yours for seizing*
My rhymes speak of love, life, and heartbreak*
They teach you how to keep believing*
My rhymes speak of happiness, sex, love and sadness*
I have a few designed for uplifting the down and grieving*
Some people find my rhymes vocally easing*
My rhymes are of truth and not always appeasing*
My rhymes speak so soothing, stress I'm relieving*

Summary**Just a little impromptu piece I decided to write after checking our credit scores. I just listen and watch what most younger people deem important. Young men choosing labels, clothing and jewelry everywhere, but they don't own what they drive or the place they lay their heads at night. Women think a high dollar bag is what life is about. Can she live in that bag? I highly doubt. Yes, it's okay to have nice things, but make wise decisions, invest in things you use. More often than not your peers are using them too. I wish

I was given that advice about investing sooner. I've never been into labels, but that was my choice. I hope in all my raw cockiness you can take something positive away. New piece written on this date 02/19/2021.

I'm Good For His Credit Score

Females running around concerned with labels*
Popping it out for anyone at a VIP table*

Sitting around looking pretty*
Wearing Dr. Miami's ass and titties*

Clothes jewelry bags and shoes*
He can't eat any of that cook your man some food*
Sucking dick to get what you want, feeling used*
Popping pussy is yesterday's news*

Times are changing*
We're all aging*
Of course, we still have sex, are you crazy?*

What else are you good for plastic whore*
I know one thing I can tell the man I adore*
I'm good for his credit score*

Dreams coming true you best believe*

At a certain age you must come clean*
Invest in shit you can redeem*
Stocks, bonds, trading and marijuana trees*
Nothing to gain wearing lashes and weave*

Invest in business, own a clothing store*
I'm good for his credit score*

I know one thing that I stay on*
Not just that dick although it's quite the schlong*
I will post the list then move along*
Equifax, Experian and Transunion*

If you don't care or agree*
Keep it moving don't mind me*

Credit score raised*
Dick follows suit my eyes are glazed*
It's called multitasking, are you amazed?*

I guess it depends what he's looking for *
But I'm good for his credit score*
Not saying he doesn't want more*
In that bedroom I'm his personal whore*
Don't get me twisted I got skills galore*
But, I'm also good for his credit score*
I said what I said now I'm shutting the door*

Summary**Some believe in spirits, ghosts or loved ones coming to visit them after they passed or they are near death. I decided to tell my experience with a story of my own. My uncle came to visit me at my job while I was later told he was on his deathbed and didn't like being in the area or on the busy street where I worked, at the time. I was also told he did not like cheese, which I did not know. He asked that I hold the cheese in his order. It felt real and it to me, was very real. I really was honored that I received that visit. I regret not getting to know my father's family better as a younger woman. My mother was supposed to make that happen when I was a child. I have so many unanswered questions now as an older woman. I'm trying now in the last few years until death to know or learn more about them through social media and various meetups. If you're my relative on my father's side of the family please feel free to reach out to me. My mind and my heart are open.

The Special Visit

The door flew open once again,
I thought more people walking in.

But, only one man appeared,
He looked familiar from ear to ear.

he had an unforgettable style,
with which he cast his daring smile.

he said how is your mother Tan,
I am the brother of your dad.

A beautiful woman you've grown to be,
was his kindly compliment to me.

I offered him something good to eat,
as he moved that toothpick between his teeth.

He said, "Sure hold the cheese. I will be right
back."
My thanks in advance for the snack.

The bag was still just sitting there,
as my manager gave me a stare.

Who did you make that order for?
My uncle, he did not go far.

I waited patiently for his return,
but I guess he decided to adjourn.

I told my family uncle Brooks came by work
today,
but for some reason he could not stay.

They stopped what they were doing work or
play,
and stared me in my puzzled face.

They said no this just can't be so,
because he died some months ago.

A strange encounter I must say,
Why was I visited this way?

From where did you come to where did you
go,
I probably will never know.

I am so honored you took time to visit me just

one more time.

Summary**These next few pieces speak volumes about love, unity and togetherness. They speak of love, soul mates, and what a wonderful mate or husband should be in his wife's, and his children's lives. I wrote about a true love that does exist, but most times can be rare. When or if you are blessed enough to find this great love, be careful to love, honor and cherish it with all you have to give. All I can say is that newlywed love should last forever. I love my man with all of me and I pray to be his forever newlywed match. These poems speak of the love that some of our grandparents shared that makes for 50+ year anniversaries. I'm talking about when he or she passed away. That can't live without them type of love. Not that we stayed together in separate rooms but slept in the bed together only when the children came for visits, types of bullshit.

Love of My Life

Love of my life, man of my dreams. This is
real or so it seems. Holding hands, bodies
interlaced, planting kisses on my face.
Morning breath, last night's sweat. It seems
we have passed the test. Doing things
together, sharing every day, we wouldn't have
it any other way. You lovin' me, I'm lovin'
you. It's obvious I love you boo. Your sexy
look, you try to cook, you made me take a
second look. I tried to write these words for
you, so that makes it impromptu. Let me know
what you think please boo. Oh, and baby
remember I Love You.

Newlyweds

He enhances me, always romances me*
Till death he's chos3n to dance with me*
I'm giddy at how he glances me*

He loves my mind body soul and heart*
He desires me, I am his peace, love and
comfort the way he ogles me I am his art*
We never unnecessarily spend a day apart*

How we met was non-traditional, yet a perfect
start*
We took vows before God now it is death do
us part*

Supportive of each other's dreams and goals*
Only reaching for one another to have and to
hold*
I write these heartfelt words for you my
husband*
I'm like no other it's my own writing flair,
Let's just call it my personal custom*
Nothing in this world will ever win against
us*
We fit together like peanuts in the shell*
You care for me like no one else*
Void of drama, void of the hell*

If we fall it's together, but still, we rise*
No fatal surprise*
We have open eyes*
We know a few are expecting our demise*

I feel safe and warm in his strong arms*
I know he will always protect me from harm*

HUSBAND

Husband is a very strong word it tells of all the responsibilities you hold upon your strong shoulders. All of the tough times we've dealt with in the past. I'm now looking forward to our fabulous future. All the love and smiles you've earned from your children and wife. You are worthy of being my husband. I truly thank you for accepting me just the way that I am. Whew!! Because I am two handfuls. For my husband I choose you and only YOU! No references needed. I trust my heart, yes that is a very important part. I also trust my instincts, and the children's input. We love the way you love and treat us. They shower you with hugs a bunch. I am your freaky lunch. Husbands lead, husbands teach; husbands love, husbands protect when we are scared/afraid. I chose you don't feel blue, a wonderful life mate, best friend, and my beautiful husband.

Wifey

When you came into my life, I tried to ignore thinking this would end up like before. A few words here and there when you see me online, maybe, but in a few conversations, you opened my mind. You allowed me into your world, told people I was your girl, claimed me in your life, protected me with all of your might. You succeeded in making me feel like your wife. My life is complete now. My heart is finally whole. Keeping you happy is my lifetime future goal. We talked, laughed, shared, and learned each other's personalities, future goals, family history, our souls/heart have grown as one. When I think of you, you then call me as if on cue. You hear my voice and just know things. I can't hide or deny anything (not that I want to) because you know me too well. You tell me you love me just when I need to hear it. No matter what people/haters tried you've reassured me you love me and only me as your woman, lover, friend, and wife. I Love how you protect all that you love, your love for your mom, my children/family and me is so amazing. I love your intelligence and the smooth way you expose people at just the perfect time, while always keeping me in the loop (No Secrets). Our relationship has withstood these tests and trials. It grows stronger daily. I once was told I just wanted to be your wife so bad, but I don't "want" to be. I already am in every way imaginable. (For Life) Your voice makes me weak and strong all at the same time. You compliment me every day. I see that many have love for you and I understand why. I love you with all the love any wife could/should have for a husband. You make me feel like no marriage license could/has ever made me feel. So, no matter what others say you are my husband (the best in my lifetime) and I am, Wifey (Forever)

Summary**This was a piece from my earlier writings. I was in a relationship with a guy that was "popular" before me. The females that he was dealing with before were simple minded and didn't know how to let go. They kept the drama going and I took to the keyboard to write about it. I would never put up with what I did then, but I was young and apparently dumb. Time really does heal all wounds.

Come Away With Me

Come away with me to our island fantasy
One without entrances or exits anyone else
can see. We'll have a password known to only
you and I. For when or if we have leave to
visit our true friends and/ or family. From the
first day you entered my world "stupid little
girls" followed with hate, drama, and strife but
I stayed your loyal friend, woman and partner
in life. I'm trying to live a happy peaceful life.
I just want to say baby you were right, the
haters most silent are not only on your end, so
for them I say our bond is really tight.
Laughing, joking, clowning, finishing each
other's thoughts and phrases, we've accepted
that we're both so crazy. I love your
everything, your voice, your laugh, and style.
The way you put your foot down in our
seldom fights, just turns me on. (Wait, that
can't be right) Then we make up and can do it
again. I knew you were the one for me. Others
threw it out to you, but you pushed past and
chose (ME) When you said you told mom
about me it spoke volumes about your feelings
for me. Everyone hears about that special one,

not random women, whores, or booty calls. People keep trying but I know they know you're my man, sweetie, and hubby on and off the net. I'm not a mean-spirited person, those that took time to know me can see. I'm so cool and sweet as can be. These stupid bitches keep me speaking my peace. Wasting their time begging, hating and pleading face it dumb BITCHES you've been (badly) defeated! Written on 1-30-2009

Summary**A minor disagreement had by a stubborn couple caused them to spend a whole night upset at each other. They were together in the same bed, but apart in their thinking and hearts, because no one would reach out to fix this disagreement. The night was equally miserable for both of them, but they just wouldn't give in. I wrote this because we have all been there. No relationship or marriage is perfect, but we should try to fix disagreements before they get out of hand.

One Horrible Night

Two hearts filled with love*
Night falls they fall asleep together cuddled up
she fits him like a glove*

Conversation flows just about the days banter*
Bills, money kids, work all it takes is one
disagreeable subject matter*

She raises her voice in defense*
He stands with power pounding his chest*

An upset couple talking no one really listening
to the other's views*
Why can't they be temporarily in each other's
shoes*

No doubt of their love, but no one backs
down*
They kept fussing and it is bedtime now*
He gets in bed turns completely around*
She notices his back to her and tears start
trickling down*

More tears and thoughts of her past
relationships ending*

Fears about what drama may be beginning*

He lays there for a while not really asleep*
Thinking I love her why don't I think before I
speak*
He wants to hold her close while he sleeps*
There's no other place she would rather be*
No one makes a move to fix this, so tonight
there will be no relief*
He falls asleep now snoring she sees this and
just lays there crying sad, and angry, in
disbelief*

She thinks about how much she loves him*
But can't make herself turn around get close
and pull him in*

She cries all night he's unaware*
She can watch him sleeping by the TV's glare*
Wanting to get close to him, but she won't
dare*

Stop fighting acting like you don't love 'em*
Life's too short so go kiss 'em and hug 'em*

What an awful night for this couple*

If this is you fix it on the double*
True Love shouldn't have all this trouble*

Summary**This is a piece about a woman having a little extra fun on the side of her marriage. It is a very descriptive piece, not for the prudish or the squeamish. I do not personally condone cheating or affairs. This piece was written as a request and I am a very open minded, non-judgmental, very creative author.

CAUGHT BETWEEN A ROCK AND A WET SPOT

It's quite sticky between that rock and that wet spot; you got me hungrily craving your taste*
Sure, my man's at home in his place, but his bedroom skills are a disgrace*

Now I'm coming to you starting anew;
Reloaded, now stride in checking me out approaching my spot*
Oh, look at what you've created wet me up sop sop*

Your tongue goes to work on my clit so lick,
suck, lick, lick*
Oh, my pussy is like a leaky faucet going drip
drip drip*
Oh yeah now it's my turn on that dick*

I'm licking it up and sucking it down, trying to
swallow it whole*
Before you stick that dick in my pussy
knocking around my organs aiming for my
soul*

Your hose wetting up my insides; I can feel
you pulsing so I'm squirting on that dick*
Oh, shit tick, tick, tick got to get home to him*

Back at home in the role of wife, cooking for
the one that brings me strife*
Thinking about how you rock my world, feed
me dick I'm hungry for life*
I got to get some more tonight*

I get showered up and lotion myself down
covered in White Diamonds fragrance a red
dress and sexy thongs*
Thinking about my beautiful sword my long
dong schlong*

How do I escape without a fight? *
I need reloading again tonight*

My hubby's at home sleepy and fed*
He doesn't seem to give a damn if I'm even in
his bed*
After dinner back to my loving I head*

I finally get back to my dick*
It seems to be waiting on me long, fat, hard
and thick*
I drop to my knees and take a wet drooling
sloppy lick*

Taking that dick in the back of my throat*
Trying like hell not to choke*

You're fucking my face*
You got my pussy squirting all over the place*

That big dick is swelling now about to
explode*
I'm ready to swallow your whole thick load*
Damn, damn, damn here it goes*

I gobble it up, got you weak your knees begin
to wobble*
Oh, just then I know it's not over you bend me

over you make me holler*

My pussy seems to swallow that dick it feels
so grand*
It need not be said you are "THE MAN" *

You're knocking on walls causing juices to run
down my legs*
Only thing competing is you giving me head*

At that moment while creaming
uncontrollably all over that beautiful dick and
you blowing another load inside of me*

Being with you has me oh so hot*
I have papers to another I almost forgot*
I'll rectify that with my legal John Hancock*
Stay in an unhappy marriage no I will not*
I realize with all this loving that I would just
forever be stuck between a rock and a wet
spot*

Summary**Just a piece where I let my art
flow from the mouth of the bong through my
fingers. It speaks on things that one may just
sit there and think about…. Something another
would just let their minds wander a bit about.

As my mind wandered, I just typed what I was thinking about. I'm sure I missed some things, but hey I have to leave some thoughts for the next great thinker….hahaha!!

WHAT IN THE BONG IS GOING ON??

Thoughts and ramblings coming from my bong*
I'm simply wondering what's going on*

It's said that God sees all*

Is that the same as the government having satellite views?*
We're down on the ground looking like ants, some of us don't have a clue*

What in the bong is going on?*
We've got "Big Brother" with cameras looking into our houses*
We've even got "Cheaters" looking into our spouses*
Yeah, I could mean the show or an actual cheater, the ones that entice him from what shows from the top of their blouses*
If God exists and he could see you now*

Tell me would you honestly feel proud?*
Like James Brown said, "Say it loud."*
Is it easy to pick out your imperfections in a
crowd?*

It's said that God knows all*

Is that the same as the government knowing
all of our business, our whole life history,
what we've said on our smartphones?
It's said that God hears all, is that how they
know what was said from the privacy of our
own homes?*
They know if we prefer Dolphin, Firefox,
Opera or Chrome*

There are many ways to talk, and many ways
to listen*
Communicating never a way to finish*

Communication is happening in many forms
without opening our mouths or actually
speaking a word*
Maybe that idea is simply absurd*
Idiotic, foolish, laughable, or inane*
Ridiculous, ludicrous, farcical, senseless,
crazy, insane*

Have you ever wondered why you can mention a food or item and the very next commercial or YouTube is pertaining to that item or food?
When no one but you is at home, are you really alone?*
Look on the TUBE it's YOU. It's YOU on the TUBE .... Hahaha YOUTUBE*
Social media is like the window to our soul, the eyes to our lives*
Side pieces sit their messaging your husbands and wives*

Looking in your friends list for faces on the book*
It's a book of many faces don't believe me, a big blue "F" just take a look*
Yes, we even share the things we eat, drink or cook*
We might as well face it our asses hooked*
Social media is the vision that lets people in*
You wonder why baby mama knows when your income tax check came in*
You buy expensive new shoes*
You haven't paid what you owe she's blowing up your phone or popping in*

Bringing baby mama blues*
Wouldn't have that problem if you'd just pay
your dues*

You can get the baby mama out your ears*
Man up and pay your arrears*

Why don't you just pay what you owe*
You sit there all day putting on an "I'm paid"
show*
Wondering how in the hell people even know*

We stay signed in keep it open day and night*
You even take it with you when you shit (I
Know Right??)*

Gross, but y'all know I am not lying*
I see your statuses when y'all break up the
whole public sees you crying*

Saying things, you know isn't real*
You know you're lying so how do you deal?*
Why not just tell us how crappy you really
feel?*
Standing in front of houses and cars posing
like it's yours*
People that are bona fide rich aren't giving
media tours*

Thieves and robbers making plans galore*
They know when you're not home of that you
make sure*
I wonder if there is social media rehab. Is
there no cure?*

It's said we're made in God's image. Is that
why we judge?*
We've got women surgically removing an
unsightly baby pudge*
Liposuctioning themselves into bottles and
jugs*

People altering pictures busy photoshopping*
Most of our women have been nose or booty
shopping*

Men committing perjury about the sizes of
their shoes*
Trying hard to convince you of what they can
do for you*
Then when time to meet in person don't know
what to do*
No need for fabrications just telling the truth*

On the net flying high*
You can be who you want it's so easy to lie*

That's not necessary, I mean really like why?*

Nothing wrong with posting things for family
and friends afar*
I think they'd be happy to see you got a new
car*
There are some serious things going on like
famine and war*
People reporting of babies being shaken,
beaten, bruised, scarred left forgotten in cars*
All this happening while we turn up and party
hard*
We think we're safe just staying at home, but
our kids can go missing just playing in the
yard*

This bong speaking truth nothing crazy*
I must admit it makes me feel a little lazy*
I'm feeling Intelligently Hazy*

Relaxes my body, and opens my mind*
Enjoy this flow soak up some knowledge read
it twice if you have time*

What in the bong is going on?*
I hope y'all stayed with me had a lot to say,
my wind was long*

I needed to pen this the need was strong*
I touched on a few things that make a person
wonder, what's going on?*
What in the bong is going on?*

Summary**** These next two poems are
about what I am as a writer, a person and a
Diva. It speaks about me as the author
Chos3nOn3Sp3aks.As a mother, grandmother,
sister, wife, friend, daughter, writer and more.
It also speaks of my past and future, my hurts
and my love. It tells of my fight and also my
scars and how I overcame them through
writing. You can also hear a live recording of
these pieces on YouTube.

https://soundcloud.com/chos3non3sp3aks/cho
s3n-diva

Chos3n Diva

Chos3n Diva I am*
Chos3nOn3Sp3aks is my personal brand*

I am strong and can make it with or without a
man*

Chos3n since first brought on earth*
It's called my birth*

Chos3n I'm responsible, the oldest of five*
Not a question or a doubt that I take no jive*

Chos3n is a mother I have four mini-ME's*
I'll take you down, if you ever mess with my
seeds*

Chos3n as a wife*
I thought that was for life*
Had to let him go, he was causing me strife*
I finally got my soldier, my soulmate, my
heart's true dclight*
When he lifts his hands to touch me it's never
to fight*

Chos3n, I was a child when my innocence was
stolen*
My father he was sick so no grudge I'll be
holding*

Chos3n put down the gun*
No need to slay nor kill for fun*

Chos3n I am the only one*
My new saga has just begun*

Chos3n to write, live, inspire*
That's my one true heart's desire*

Chos3n has ups and downs*
Helps me relate to smiles and frowns*

Chos3n wears many hats in a day*
Still the royal crown is here to stay*

Chos3n has love all around full and free*
God blessed me with my family*
Chos3n knows God does love she*
"He's Got Me! He's Got Me!" I shout proudly*
Chos3n is vocally free, high spirited simply
put you'll love just plain old me*

Chos3n knows mothers' woes*
Issues so bad had me pulling on my Afro*
I asked, "Lord please show me the way to
go"*
I'm a survivor*
Chos3n is diverse*
A mentally strong striver*

Chos3n was the past I had; I won that fight*

Prayed to God almighty said he'd made it alright*
Hurry get your shades, see my future is bright*
Check out Chos3n bumping elbows with the stars side by side*
She's smiling bright sharing Diva spotlight*

Take It from A Diva

A Diva I is, A Diva I am*
Not correct grammar, but trust me when I'm done you won't give a damn*
I won't borrow or steal yo man*
He read my words fantasized my skills and said damn*
Tapped me on my page with, "Can I peek your brain ma'am?" *

First, they say I'm a cutie*
That my man is in luck about that booty duty*

Look man I don't believe in luck*
I just know when he needs to be loved sucked or fucked*

Although I can sometimes be rude or crass*

I am an intelligent woman of class*
Just saying when I'm done, he's going to
remember my ass*
He says, "I see you put it down for your
man"*
Can you talk to my woman, invite her to your
class?*
I love her but she got limits on the ass*
That's not my place*
He should tell her to her face*
She'll be wounded at first, then consider her
options with style and grace*
Knowing he can get it some other place*
Cook for him, feed him berries and grapes*
Try pole dancing suck him right get your
tongue in place*
When he squirts, you'll be loving his taste*
You're going to be happy to ride his face*
Cause with my man I'll win first place*
I got much class don't want your space*

I'm never insecure*
Chos3n's confident for sure*
I'll share some tools and knowledge with you*

No need to be swift no need to be strong*
It's your schlong work it all night long*

Just do him right no shame to your game*
That's your man, don't you wear his name?*

If you find it gross or hard to do*
You're with the wrong man he's not meant for
you*
Take it how you want because I speak the
truth*

When love is real there's no need for disguise*
He'll know you want him from the look in
your eyes*

That attraction to please him can't be faked or
denied*
You'll view him with pride, he's your king
forget his shoe size*
He'll see you as beauty no matter your size*
He won't need excuses or alibis*
He'll rush home to you spring open them
thighs*
She'll suck it and swallow with a gleam in her
eyes*
Coming home to you is not what he should
despise*
Just a word to you ladies hold his heart you'll

have his eyes*
Yes, when they come to me, I feel some
pride*
Of all the compliments I admire that I'm
lyrically wise*
He tells me thanks and that he will give wifey
a fair try*
I tell him goodbye, because I value my own
love, my man, hubby he's a heck of a prize*
the apple of my eye*

https://soundcloud.com/chos3non3sp3aks/ta
ke-it-from-a-diva

Summary**This next piece is a lot more
than just a slightly silly adult piece. It uses the
five senses. It's a fun, silly, sensual, sexy read.
It does have serious notes of
appreciation, gratefulness and it is quite
descriptive.

An Insomnia Tale

I am awake again another night. This not
being able to sleep is really not the business. I

lie there next to you I can (SMELL) you I inhale your woodsy cologne scent. It is really just waking me up more my body is aroused. I lie on my tummy with my head up just to look at you. Admiring the good man that you are. I (SEE) you, I am just watching your sexy ass sleep. I (HEAR) you, I am listening to you snore. (That's not so sexy...lol) Still I am thanking God for the simple gifts he's bestowed to my life. Yes, you are definitely one of those gifts; Since the night is young. I reluctantly tear myself from your strong, warm, loving arms. I walk through the house to check on the children. I go into the children's rooms. I love watching their tummies going up and down. I watch them sleep, watching them for a few minutes resting peacefully I (TOUCH) my lips to their heads and plant kisses on top. Thanking God for all the unique personalities that make each their own person. *(To Hubby) Back in your arms I'm still awake, insomnia is ruling me, I lay next to you touching your body as you sleep. You are always so hot, not warm, actually feverish. I just love you so much.* How did I get blessed to have my soulmate, lover, friend, husband to spend this lifetime with? How did I end up with this stubborn, manly man that still looks at me with adoration, like I am the most beautiful, sexiest woman he has ever seen? I also can't believe he seems happy to have me for his very own. A man that puts up with my many bossy sprees, controlling rampages, or mental ailments. He understands that my horrific past has made me who I am, and he loves me anyway. I ask God to let me calm down enough not to run him away, to know/trust him to do what he is supposed to do for this family. Also appreciate continuing to be blessed and happy and thanking God time has gone by. I look at the clock and realize it is only about one hour before time to wake hubby for work. I leave his arms once more, then I crawl down kissing his belly, finally down to his manhood I (TASTE) him, I taste his dick until it hardens and human caramel pours from the top. I roll my tongue around it. I suction my mouth up and down it, enjoying my candy as if I was starting a strict new diet within the next hour or so. I can taste his salty excitement causing my pussy to drip. Causing his dick to harden more. Rock hard is a good way to say it. What did I start here that dick looks scary? I try to push it deeper into my throat, challenge accepted. Ohhhh shit it fits. I taste it now sweet, happy about the fruit you have been eating lately. I began to run my tongue ring along the balls then up to the head and then the entire shaft, He exploded then it began to melt. I lick clean every drop of my delicious caramel, then look up to his beautiful smiling face and I (HEAR)Good morning Bea-u-ti-full! I smile then head to the bathroom. I come back with a warm towel in my hand for him and say Good morning Poppa, still licking him off of my lips. I cleaned him up before tasting him one last time.

Summary**This piece was a written request for a man I was getting to know at that dating stage of my life. He sent me some pictures and after finding out I was a writer, he asked me to write something for him describing what I thought of his pictures after I saw them. He wanted to read my impromptu work so he put a short time limit on when he wanted to see the completed poem. This is

what I came up with in about twenty minutes.
Some of the feelings are quite embellished
because I really did not know him that well. It
was fun to write though.

Your Pictures

A plethora of pix, a timely mix*
I've had the awesome pleasure of being sent*
From a handsome man after some lovely
phone time, we spent*

At first glance a compliment I sung*
I admit DAMN you look so handsome and
young*
I can tell by your words you desire more than
just games and fun*

I understood fully when you said the one you
seek, would lock eyes with you then all the
pains of life you've been through, she'd
understand and see*
No need for words no need for speech*
Seeds have been planted for your hand she'd
always reach*

Got off the subject of the pictures for a while*

All things included I like your style*
Did you blush when I said thanks your
pictures all look divine?*
You don't look like a man of the mature age
you claim to me you look Hella fine*
Lick my lips a tad bit naughty, but you just
don't look like you're over forty*

A few pictures struck me as you look a little
mean*
That voice of yours was so serene*

This poem however impromptu*
Written all for you*
I'm honored just hope you like it too*

Your eyes appear to be looking deep into me,
piercing my soul*
No worries for me I have nothing to hide if
you become mine, keeping you happy will be
my ultimate goal*

About this piece I ask your honest thoughts*
Because from my heart I write this it was not
learned nor taught*

I believe people enter our lives for a reason,

season, or lifetime, so it's all predestined if
you will be mine*
We will definitely know with more time*

I'm laughing now cause all of this seems
funny*
I may have just written this piece for my
future hubby*

Summary**“No More” Was the first piece
I wrote that made me know that writing was
my thing. That writing was my gift. I gave this
to my abusive ex-husband and I felt
empowered. He didn’t take heed to my
writing, hence the reason he is no longer my
husband. This piece was also shared and I was
told has helped many women. It is the answer
to abuse of any kind because I nor you are
going to take it anymore. NO MORE, NO
MORE, NO MORE!!

NO MORE!! (Revised)

NO MORE, will I sit and accept your
belittling and criticisms. I am the one YOU
chose to share your life, and children with. I

am the other half of the parenting equation, and I will NOT remain silent. I have earned and deserve respect, love and appreciation. NO MORE will I allow the children to be called beneath their names, out of their names, or the names that you are portraying yourself as, such as wimpy, idiot, lazy, or good for nothing. What you speak doesn't make you more of a man. It makes you so small you can't even see yourself. NO MORE will I be ignored when asking a question, ALL questions from me are and should be important enough to receive an answer. NO MORE late-night cries while you rest your eyes in sleep unaware, or do you even care what is going on around you? NO MORE will heads be bowed, and looking down, while you are lecturing, speaking, or disciplining our children. God has given them to us to build up, not to tear down. They will be taught to walk with their heads high and not down in shame even if I have to encourage and raise them alone. NO MORE will things go so far that there is no returning without the breaking of someone's spirit. NO MORE will there be a control demon in this house. I chastise all evil and negative feelings and vibes from this house. NO MORE will a fantasy (porn) be used to tear down your real life loving, caring, beautiful (inside and out) wife. You married me, I had your babies, I put up with your ways, your dirty laundry, your bad moods, your morning breath, just you period…. and now it's me that isn't your ideal anymore. (Wake up MAN!!) NO MORE will I not be supported or appreciated for the good I do to make things better for my family. NO MORE will you or should you allow your family to be tampered with or stolen away from you by whatever hindrance you deem more important than your family, to take you back to that empty lonely shell you once were. NO MORE will men order or tell their spouses what they can and cannot do, what to wear, and where they can or cannot go. Love, honor and respect her and she will do what is pleasing in the eyes of God, and she will enjoy doing things that please YOU, her husband the person she promised herself to till death. NO MORE will financial decisions be for a man, and dishes, and laundry be a woman's work. We are and should be equal life partners sharing everything. NO MORE will you allow any distractions to not let you be the man that follows God so your family can look up to you and be proud. NO MORE will you walk through the door, and let the negativity of the world fill your head with distaste and disgust for coming home to your family. NO MORE will there be evil or unclean distractions. Unnecessary distractions that could/would keep you locked away in your own world alienating your family or loved ones. NO MORE will your head be filled with the lies or notions that you are too tired or busy to do something with or spend time with your family. You're never too tired to roll with your friends/your boys whatever name they go by. NO MORE will communication not be welcomed in this house. NO MORE will you think of certain children as MY children, and not our children. NO MORE will the way we were raised be the base for our mistakes, we have the power to change this. NO MORE will we have a problem hugging, or showing love to all of our children, because our parents didn't show us how. NO MORE will we risk everything worth having (including our souls)

for one night we think no one will ever know about. NO MORE will any of this foolishness or negativity be tolerated in this house. This house is God's house, and I am taking it back. NO MORE will the world or anything negative or damaging have that kind of power over this family, our family. NO MORE, NO MORE, NO MORE. I Speak these things in the name of the almighty God. I thank God for everything he has done and the strength he has given me to speak these words to someone that was abusing his family, marriage and relationships.
Written By: Chos3nOn3Sp3aks in 2000

Summary**Warning: this is only art. Do not resort to violence of any kind. I do not recommend any violence ever!!! Don't call the police. This piece is just a little look inside of every woman's mind at some point in her life (AKA PMS and a trifling man at the same

time). The poem was written to the extreme.
More extreme than we would actually imagine
unless we were at our highest point of anger,
but these are only thoughts so PLEASE,
DON'T DO IT????

Dangerous!!!!

I could threaten to cut off your balls and choke
you with them in your sleep, but what good
would it do you'd still lie to me? I could
threaten to poison your food, do you bodily
harm, but it still wouldn't change that you're a
dirty dog. I could cut your tires, bleach your
whole wardrobe, leave you without a stitch of
clothes, pull a "Left Eye" and set your place
on fire, but it still would not change my true
heart's desire. I could key your car, be a fatal
attraction, whip your ass like I'm Joe or
Action Jackson, but I'll never understand
men's dumb actions. I could join forces with
Madea only with a few minor changes. Bake a
sweet potato pie? No!! My grilled cheese will
tame you. I'll do a few little things that will
drive you crazy, but harming you is harming

me, still doesn't explain why you lie to me. You can call me crazy, I'll claim that, but it seems you are my crazy equal match. This is a little insight to most women's minds, so stop playing games man; don't you think it's time? Lying, deceiving, playing sneaky games, playing with women's emotions thinking it's OK. Let's see if you make it to a ripe old age. If love and hate are the same emotion then I hate you to death, what a scary notion. My brain is a time bomb going tic tic tic, welcome to the mind of your little lunatic. Love You

Summary**This is from some internet beef in my younger days. I was a mean and angry little thang. I also had a good for nothing guy that didn't speak up so I thought I should do it on my own. Now I know that we were both wrong. I just want to show the power of the pen. You can slay with words and I was getting it in, or was I? "Just Cause I Can Do That SHIT!!"

Just Cause I Can Do That SHIT!!

I'm just venting on MY page 'cause I can do that shit. Some of this internet shit makes me angry first then my Tango Etude kicks in and gets your asses laid out. Whether it be from the verbal blow I threw that knocks you the fuck out. My real people can roll in and wild out. Either way your dumbasses find yourself laid out. I'm online just to have some fun. My little 4"11 ass is cocky. I know I can write my ass off. Also, I know I have the best man for me. I'm happy as fuck. No, I'm not rich. I have issues just like you, but I have love from my man and children so I definitely have riches that some will never understand. Even when they drive me crazy or get on my last nerve, I love them. They are loyal to me and not going anywhere. Yes, hoe I mean the man also. He's SPRUNG so stop prancing around in your undies waiting for us to invite you over cause you're NOT our type. I know my man's page LQQKS demonic, he always calling y'all bitches and he's mean as hell to y'all but you dumb ass hoes stay on his friend list, so while I sit on his dick reading emails from you trying to give him pussy. I wonder why you bitches just don't delete yourselves. I guess you simply enjoy abuse, you're stupid or your just in denial.

Summary**The next piece was written
About an abusive relationship I and my
children were in. I did not feel strong enough,
nor know how to get out. I gradually started to
get stronger, got my finances stronger and got
us out of there. It took longer than I wanted it
to, but I did what I could do for the situation I
was in and the money that I had, to be able to
start over and take care of my four children.
It's hard to be a stay home mom because you
don't make money to pay bills. Daycare costs
too much. It feels like you're stuck. I know
someone may be in this situation right now.
There is help out there. Try Faith House or
another women's abuse center near you
PLEASE? It does not matter how you do it,
just please get out. No one else can understand
or judge how or why you did what you did,
but that is not what is important. You living to
see another day is the ultimate goal. Abusers
will prey on anyone in a weaker position than
they are. A weaker position being anything
they can use to control you such as: financial,
size, gender, lack of education, mental...etc. I

wrote this from a fact and fiction point of view
I added some things to the poem to make it
flow.

I Took It Then...Try It Again??
Why did I mistake the fury of your fist,
for a loving kiss?*
How weak was I to let you do this?*

Why did I make your ass lunch after every
brutal punch? *
How weak was I to love you that much?*

Why did I mistake your yelling for loving?*
Or maybe it was the kicking and the
punching*
Let's not forget all the others you bragged
about fucking*

The binge eating had me packing on more
pounds*
More of me led to more fighting and boxing
rounds*
Was it my fault that you constantly threw me
on the ground?*
Why did I let you bring me down?*

You were pulling on my hair, no not in that sexy way*
Dragging me back in the house telling me that I could go, but forcing me to stay*
"No one will want you, you are fat with too many kids", He would say*

How do I get blamed cause another man is looking at me?*
Maybe you should take another look to see what he sees?*
Why did I stay when you didn't appreciate me?*

Aww how sweet I thought of you to act so jealous?*
For you I was stupid and truly zealous*

That jealousy suddenly stopped being so cute, after you slapped me so hard, I actually lost a tooth*
You had all of the children watching you act a fool*
Maybe you weren't acting, that's just what you do?*
Your size 12 shoe was good for nothing, but

stomping me black and blue*
What the fuck was I doing?*
No time for me to sit there boo-hooing*
Life is too short. I had to get my life moving*

When you struck one of the kids*
I finally flipped my fucking lid*
I had to stop and say oh no that's it*
We had done nothing to deserve that shit*
Nothing at all I wasn't going to put them
through any more of this*

I am good for something you'd soon
remember numbers stuck in my head*
You a crazy motherfucker that will be
penniless once you lay down for bed*

Online I was shrinking your $$ I'm so
amazing*
I emptied your checking and went for your
savings*

Into my account I transferred it all*
I pictured every punch and kick as my account
grew big and tall*
What are you going to do about it? Punch in
another wall?*

Not at this house because you'll be gone, me
and the kids will have a ball*
Speaking of balls, I have them all*
Yes, your sorry dick took a major fall*
Wasn't great anyway and I'm not talking just
small*
You woke me up for the last morning with a
final face hit*
Once you leave for work today that will be it.
*

A new day has begun, all locks changed by
Mr. Locksmith*
Have you forgotten that this is my shit*
Surprise, surprise nigga you got your last, git*
Your meager wardrobe is out by the ditch*
I just got you back for me and all those other
women you hit*
Walked around here Mr. I'm running shit*
When I'm done with your Social, you'll be
slitting your wrists*
Whoa, hey what you reaching for, hopefully
not your dick?*
You have just been neutered you useless
prick*

Summary**This is a love poem about an

ex that used to call me "Angel". I had to leave the state where he was, and temporarily be separated from him. I was away out of state for some time. Many people including his exes tried to come between us. The relationship wasn't strong enough to survive the separation, so the women eventually succeeded in breaking us up. It is written as a comparison where I am the fish and he is the water.

Fish Out of Water

I'm a freshwater fish and you are my water. I've been sent here to this saltwater. I'm slowly dying oh the horror. Getting doses of freshwater every day is the only thing holding me here alive and awake. Sustaining me daily cause you see I'm swimming straight to you, as you slowly continue rolling away. You attract other fish along the way; old fish, new fish, stank fish, ewww fish, fish that you have thrown back, fish that have been thrown back time and time again by others. All are trying to distract you from nurturing me. I'm dying little by little daily can't you see? I'm flapping around trying to wrap myself in thee. I love you freshwater, don't you leave. Must I mention how you once came and swept me off my fins, cared for me, loved and married me, your angelfish undoubtedly. You should be stagnant without me and I should be dead without you. Let's not end up a travesty. Your fish is waiting on her living waters, but to you seems I'm now a bother. Ultimatums, Oh and bossy is what you call me not taking time to see that this little fish truly loves and needs thee. All the other fish that's been in your waters could care less if you were gone tomorrow, dried out evaporated it wouldn't phase them but I know I couldn't take it. They like showing out, causing trouble, not a care if you lose out because they already got what they got. Here I am your Angelfish with all I have. No, it's not much but it's so real worth more than theirs. You are my last, my all, my everything. My offer to you is ME. I love you freshwater.

Summary**No one wants to nor deserves to be called crazy for the way they are or feel about certain things. Things happen in life that are the reason all of us are the way we are, be that positive or negative. I just felt if someone was going to call me crazy let me not make a liar out of him/her. Am I crazy? No. Could I be that? Hell yeah. I hope you enjoy this next piece

Crazy ????(I Got That)

Hell, you say I'm crazy and I need counseling NEWSFLASH: The shrink offered me a position to sit in on groups and help others. With all I've been through I'm thinking I should be crazier than this? Am I crazy because I was molested by my natural father from the ages of two to ten? Am I crazy because men came into my mom's life and tried the same thing time and time again? Maybe I'm crazy because my mom didn't do anything about it because she really wanted to keep her man around. I may be crazy because I was expected to put my mouth on a penis before the age of eleven against my will? You constantly say I'm crazy, but have you ever questioned why? Could it be that no matter what kind of woman I've been, by giving in to the flexibilities and wild freaky antics of my partner; while catering to all their needs they still cheated on and abused me physically and verbally? I know what makes me crazy is being/feeling disrespected or used by people that supposedly love me? Maybe it's the sexual violations "rapes" that make me so crazy, not sure just asking? I probably should be crazy straight jacket wardrobe and all because of that one time I threw a Nike and you claim it hit you or even the times I told you if you ever cheated on me I would "cut your dick off" Can I be deemed crazy when I'm washing your feet, cooking your meals, licking and sucking you all over, caring for the children, holding down jobs that it takes special training/skills to do, getting an education beyond High School, even got a job working w/kids, no criminal record ever, listening to your issues and offering insightful advice that you most times used. Maybe it's me being supportive loving your kids and mine the same. I may be crazy for knowing you too well what you like/want/need keeping order everywhere never letting anyone run over me/us. All I do, think about, live, respect, love, care for, talk about, look forward to is you and our future, so yes, I'll admit it I'm crazy alright. Crazy about YOU and what we're building and if you even get a notion to leave or be without me that would make you crazier than me. Now what????

Summary**** This next piece is simply about the world we live in. The news reports of so many Negative things. Try to tune it out but I just can't it's hard having such a big, warm heart in this cold-hearted world. Just read it, no further explanation needed.

COLD HEARTED WORLD

Our eyes are opened but still we don't see, all of the people in need*
We have a great deal to give but stand here always ready to receive*
We share nothing it's just our personal greed*
People are screaming, but it sounds like whispers, so we don't hurry nor heed*
It should be heartbreaking, painful but we are cold so that we don't grieve*
Eat glass for breakfast, tough as nails no problems we don't bleed*
Death all around us, young, old, babies, kids, we are uncaring and cold, so we don't grieve*
Am I my brother's keeper, of course I am but that I don't believe*

It takes to much heart so that information my
mind refuses to retrieve*
It's truly simple, but that would take too much
time out of our selfish lives to perceive*
We'd rather look the other way grab our
mocha lattes keys, smartphones and just
leave*
Life is a boxing match we've perfected the bob
and weave*
We don't have respect for our own spouse we
run around playing the field to or own we
don't cleave*
Our children are growing up with us in their
view, but no one to show, guide, or lead*
They don't grow up like us when times were
love in families*
We were taught right from wrong by the
village some had whole communities*
In a world of technology, they don't see what
they should be, they've no respect for thee*
STOP!! Take some time to show some love*
This world needs The Almighty One above*
Do you know of whom I speak?*
Seems like none of us does:(

Summary**These are more mental health

awareness pieces. I truly feel like it may be some of the more relatable pieces that I've written. 2020 has been a very different year for everyone. It has been many different things for many different people, some positive, some negative, but more importantly it has enhanced and brought mental health to the forefront of awareness more than ever before. I am bi-polar (mania), Obsessive Compulsive Disorder, agoraphobia, and panic/anxiety attacks. Writing really helps me with my mind's chemical imbalance. This event actually happened. I tried my best to vividly describe my mental breakdown. I hope this helps someone or if any of this seems relatable, maybe it can lead you to talk to someone. Please take care of your health and that includes your mental health.

Breaking Point

Yesterday I had a breakdown*
My mental wasn't sound*
My mind in a negative space my happy was not found*
Mentally discombobulated things were strewn around*

I was not myself I did not laugh or clown*
I did not wish to talk to anyone in town*
Thought I'd feel better after the call from
mom*
Too far-gone tick tick tick, my nearest loved
one experienced my emotional bomb*

Wanted to shut down my mind*
Today I'm feeling fine*
I just needed and took a little time*
Will it happen again? I don't know I will not
lie*
I can't promise anything but I'll certainly try*

I was burdened feeling peaked*
It was serious, tears were leaked
Brain was busy answers were seeked*
I had questions, but no answers honestly all I
felt was defeat*
Didn't care for things to eat*
Time was too busy for sleep*
I felt useless, I felt weak*
I wanted to disappear, retreat*
Go back to a baby on mom's teat*
Can't explain it, but it was deep*
Was it really quite so bleak*

Writing is calming I feel complete*
Being in control is a daily feat*

Laugh to keep from crying*
The dam bursts, so I cried to keep from dying*
No finality, dark thoughts, ending it, all am I
Implying*
There's no coming back from the grave, no use
trying*
I can always come back from the tears I'm
drying*
Living with, death, sadness, secrets and lying*
Life is way harder than some think *sighing*

Every day is not so good, I'm working on me*
Open up talk to someone no need to be
discreet*
There are days I don't want to talk to anyone at
all not even my friend down the street*
Mental health awareness needs way more than
a month or a week*
All days are not cheerful, I pray for upbeat*
Bipolar depression does not have me beat*
I'll try again tomorrow as the new day I greet*
I suffer from Bipolar depression, anxiety, and
OCD*
Welcome to the world of Chos3nOn3Sp3aks*

You Won't Win So Don't Do It

Dangerous combination you know this is true*
Battle with your woman is this what you really
want to do? *

Wiser men have done it stupid at its best*
They said that unspeakable thing that lands
them in the room used by family or guests*
Don't you ever compare me to your ex*
For any man that's an awful mess*
Remember for me to be like her we'd have to
erase the sex*
Also remember while you were working, she
was probably somewhere bent over; behind a
revolving door where she yelled, "NEXT!"

Before you compare me remember this is
where from the start you said you wanted to
be*
Better watch yourself when you try to come
for me*
I'm Chos3n and no one else can ever be she*

Before you compare me to anyone*
Remember that pedestal you put me on could

get kind of heavy trying to hold up more than
one*
You got to put down the others; their dead
POW POW smoking gun*
Being the woman, I am makes me a hot
commodity, nothing new this hasn't just
begun*
With me you get it all and not just a little or
some*
With me you'll get love, great conversation,
laughter and fun*
You can talk slick if you like, but we both
know I come second to none*

Don't come off slick with me bridle your
tongue control what comes out*
I know I've said my share I admit it no doubt*
You should know when you're hitting to low,
I mean I'm an erotic writer what is this really
about*
I'm still the one that has you floating high and
weak at the same time with only my mouth*
I also know you can't resist what I'm holding
down south*
Yeah, look at it stop drooling don't you love
how she pouts*

She's dried now all your fault from vile words
that you spout*
Sasha could be squirting, it's your fault that
she's not*
You spoke stupid bullshit that got Trouble
kicked out*

You tried to shoot shit at me shots fired,
attack, venom, poison*
Of that I am the baddest, insults, attacks, I
have plenty you know foison*

Hope you felt bigger trying to hurt my
feelings*
Nice job, but you shouldn't forget I'm the
woman with whom you have a lifetime of
dealing*

Either love me or leave me because you can't
do both*
This is not one of my cute, little love notes*
There are choices before you. Chos3 wisely I
hope*
I need an apology no it's not a joke*
Let's see what you bring then Sasha and I can
take a vote*
This piece isn't anything like the others I

wrote*
I'm not upset or mad maybe a little hurt*
Just remember you took it to that level first*
Not trying to open the door for those dudes
filled with thirst*
My love is so big my heart threatens to burst*
It's true that loving someone can sometimes
be a curse*
Disagreements with loved ones are truly the
worst*
Whoa look at me slaying as I'm killing each
verse*

Even with my issues medically speaking*
Nothing any woman can do that I can't never
defeating*
This war with me you shouldn't be seeking*
You compared me to someone that in bed is a
lazy, fat, I don't do that, weakling*

I bring it sexy and that's no lie*
She couldn't measure up no matter how hard
she ever tried*
Chronic suffering and discomfort aside*
There's something addicting about my kind of
pie*
Do you wish to challenge, do you wish to

deny?*
You brought the tear, but you didn't make me cry*
The ball is in your court so what's up guy?*
You inspired this write while I'm naked and high*
LMAO my my my*
I hope you're upstairs thinking oh why, oh why?*
Hopefully soon you'll apologize*

Summary**This piece is basically me wanting some one-on-one special time with my man and not being too afraid to ask for what I want. We work together, live together and are almost always around or close to each other, but we are usually doing our own things. I might be reading, creating, writing, sewing, exercising, or watching television…etc. upstairs; While he may be playing games, doing dishes/laundry or watching television…. etc. downstairs. No lie he spoils me and caters to my wants and needs, but I want more time. I guess it's loving greed. If I don't state it, he won't be aware of the need. I hope you enjoy the piece.

SP3AK UP K33P UP!

When I want his time there's no game, I just state it*
Keeping our relationship tight and connected, I'm elated*
I don't like arguing but if he's slipping, I'll debate it*
I'm asking for some time so focus and make it*
Stop everything else I demand he create it*
Go the extra mile I'll give back, but I'll definitely take it*
I'm aged my knowledge refined; trust me he doesn't hate it*

If I'm asking for time just trust that I need it*
Keep the outside to a minimum, relationship undefeated*

I've been through too much with lames, with him I've upgraded*
He gave me time and more to gain this*
He's got to keep that same energy and more to maintain it*

My past is no comparison he's a beast, my
problems he ate it*
Ready and willing if a lame thought crazy and
retaliated*
My life was hell, stress crumbled, all gone like
cheese he grated*
My past done, we're together I'm so elated*
I said that to say, all negative shit dissipated*

We've gained a routine over the years*
I try not to let things switch too many gears*
I've shared my life with people expelling too
many tears*
I no longer own those issues, problems or
fears*
You are definitely it for me my dear*

I'm wiser now and I know my worth*
I also know that you elevated my past life and
swept out the dirt*
I shouldn't feel pain, I don't deserve to hurt*
We've been in this too long, and it has always
worked*
If we see some slack, we should be able to
report*
We need to talk relationship alert*
Reign us in, speak it out, show each other

support*
Circle kept small, a two-person fort*

I'll be your peace*
We can breathe with ease*
Communication and action give us sweet release*
Let's talk it out as I rub your feet*
Relationship tight no spot left open, not a chance for an outsider to enter or squeeze*
Not a place for a thot or nigga to seize*
If we didn't want to be here, we'd be free there's no leash*
No fighting in these streets*
What's mine is for me*
Nobody out of character, no one is losing teeth*
I'm happy and cared for no need for lost sleep*
I'm not new to relationships, men have tried and offered I passed on it, leave*
I love all of him, not parts, not a piece*
My inbox is popping go away from me please*
I'm not tempted nor teased*
I'm not flattered by flirting, trust and believe*
I get that and more at home happiness

achieved*
Much attention at home love, spoiled and free
from disease*
Not faking, or acting what you get is what you
see*
Long-term couple goals we will forever be*
Your Erotic (Relationship) Queen*
I'm Chos3nOn3Sp3aks*

Summary**This poem steams from almost
everything I write about. I've been through a
lifetime of drama, relationships, issues,
arguments, situations, scenarios...etc. in my
life and I've come through a queen. Do I feel
like I can help anyone on the relationship tip?
Yes, I've learned enough to know what works
and what does not. I've played with one's not
faithful, allowed others to join, I've found my
place desiring love wanting it all. I personally
require longevity, faithful, caring, funny,
loving, intelligent, but will still beat the brakes
off of any motherfucker that tries to hurt, harm
or disrespect me. I've had men that I've gone
to war for that wouldn't even play fight for
me. I've counseled, people needing advice,
I've set their relationship straight. I'm not

licensed and I don't need to be my life scars
and lessons are my certified degree. Think
very hard on what you have is he a life mate
or a throwaway? Don't fret fellas the King's
Edition is right below so continue reading.

Erotic Relationship Queen

Self-professed erotic Relationship Queen*
Doesn't make it any less true, that I'm self-
deemed*
I share instructions galore time to spill the
beans*
First things first never cause a seen*

Never lower yourself to his loser level*
I know it hurts I've been there before, but
handle this correctly be more clever*
Remain a queen remember your character, flip
a coin good or evil*
Long handled spoon, protect your heart handle
him like a devil*
He may try to return after you pull the lever*
Like dirt on your shoes keep returning throw
them away you can do better*
Please don't take him back he's shown who he
is let him go now and forever*

You should tell him you will return to him in 2000 and never*
A good man is simple it does not take all of that*
Morals, values, a heart of gold, that is the ground he stands*
If you don't want him, he may be hurt or sad*
He won't try to pressure or brow beat you he'll just wave his hand*
He's ready for love and most times he will marry the next queen he lands*
Your loss read about it your heart has been slammed*

Ready or not a good man can't be tested by your friends*
Don't try that shit he'll have you questioning them*
A good man will hear you when you talk and talk*
He's listening filling his good man vault*
He may smoothly remind you when you don't walk the walk*

He won't argue or create rifts*
He'll give you meaningful made for you gifts*
He loves family, games, and peace*

You're his family, be his peace, I have a game
suck him to sleep*
Wake him up let him eat, then you can fuck
him weak*

You don't have to track him down*
He won't be in the streets running around*
Not out with his boys acting like clowns*
This man is a king he knows to whom he is
bound*

Dating, married, or engaged*
He's faithful to you at any stage*

Your man should come before your friends*
Don't share too much of your business with
them clucking hens*
Oh, you mad? If they are true, a friend will
respect and be there in the end*

You shouldn't have to keep your man from
anyone*
If he violates in any way girl high tail it and
run*
If you can't trust him it's over y'all done*

You may ruin him by handling him like your
previous man*

We should know that each person deserves his
own chance*
Learn yourself know what you won't accept,
self-romance*
Be honest with yourself. Do you really want a
good man? *
Are you bound to the loser that fucked your
aunt Fran?*
He's not going to change girl please
understand*

Bet you still want Jamal cause he's so fine*
I mean he only fucked your cousin and aunt
Fran one time*
Okay that's it I tried*
You keep trying to resuscitate when this
relationship has died*
This queen has things to do, so all I'm saying
is GURL BYE!!

Summary**I wrote this next piece on the
spot. It's not as detailed as I would like it to
be, but I'm sure a King could read it and find
his true Queen. It and the one before it was
freestyle written especially for this book. Raw
no re-dues. I hope you enjoy them both.

EROTIC RELATIONSHIP QUEEN
(King Edition)

Hey there King I'm back again*
Heed my words if you came to win*
Grab a drink, get comfy, erotic relationship
queen on ten*
Whatever you like Vodka, Remy or Henn*
You may be one of the rowdy kings that drink
Gin* (Watch this one ladies)
You know they say it makes you sin*

Okay first of all if you call a woman bitch, she
will be that bitch*
She'll be nice and loving until you flip that
switch* (DON'T DO IT!)

There should be words a true king would
never utter*
Disgusting would make a true queen shudder*
Leave all that trashy talk in the gutter*
You need to show her your smooth as butter*
Woo her like there is no other*

She should trust you and love you, with a
smiling embrace*

You protect her, you love her, you make her
feel safe*
She should be your peace, your power, your
grace*
She should be forever around you sharing
your space*
She should dance for you wearing flowers and
lace*
Breasts dropping on your mouth, let's taste*
Pussy popping on your throne like the #1,
ace*
Popping it up and down, twirling hips,
muscles pulsate*
King can you hear me? Are you awake? *
Like Tony said, "They're GREAT!!*
The mess her pussy is making called a
beautiful disgrace*
Why such a disgustingly happy look on your
face*

King if she isn't your biggest cheerleader, then
she isn't your woman*
The woman for you puts you second to none*

Second only breeds trouble*
Shut that shit down on the double*

Side chicks, side dudes*
Kings and queens don't deem these phrases
cool*

Your home and all inside should meet your
personal expectations*
Your queen by your side adding her own burst
to the creation*

You should be home for peace*
Home is your retreat*
Home, Oh man your sweet release*
No need to sneak*
She'll meet your needs*
Love should exceed*
Dick hard, quite free from disease*
Your dreams are her dreams*
Vice versa, supportive indeed*
A woman for her king will always drop to her
knees*
She would suck him and fuck him, fulfill
every need*
Cooking can be shared different options are
eased*
If you keep things simple both easily
appeased*

If she works home chores is both of your
jobs*
But a working man is sexy, so more slob for
your nob*
She may like sports or she may not*
By your side or on your lap try leaving her a
spot*

Women remember every little thing*
What she interprets from you is the noise she
will bring*

Take her out with you or she'll call you a
cheater*
A good woman won't fuck another if she feels
you don't need her*
She knows her worth and she's out of their
quick as if you'd beat her*

Respect breeds respect*
She will shower you with her breasts…*
LMAO I meant best*
She's all yours there is no rest*
You won't go home to any tests*
She knows you treat her best*
No questions, answers, guess*
She trusts you she's loyal what else is left*

Maybe married, maybe not*
Maybe he has a plan, maybe he forgot*

She's expecting a visual win to your
relationship, you better not play*
That piece of paper you must display*
On your knee double down, prove your hand,
parlay*
Simpler than we agree to every day*
If men understood women most relationships
would slay*

King you got this I believe in you, a rare
breed*
You can have your pick look beyond the thots,
whores and sleaze*
Make it to the good woman please*
Men confuse good with the skeeze*
Kings prefer travel and skis*

She'll lift you up show support*
Be the only lady you desire to court*
Make dinner plans and become dessert*
Fuck you suck you slurpity slurp*
Not a lot like her on this earth*
She'll do her part* Never come in short*
Laugh at the silly, her smile tugs at your

heart*
Quite simple actually she wants this to start*
Attention, food, laughter, she loves
completing your better part*

King you know the signs if she's is not loyal*
Never treats you royal*
Too many men in her life, she has let soil*
They fucked her then separated like water and
oil*
Disrespected she was left with their babies to
struggle and toil*

If this is the life she keeps choosing*
Downright crazy and abusing*
You can't find yourself, lowering your crown
losing*

She is not yours king*
Find the one that aligns within you, bring*
Find the one who wears your heart and ring*
Find the one that will toil with you through
anything
Her crown was sloping this is nothing for you
King
Straighten that crown rejoice man sing*
all done now, guess what/ You chose a Queen

surely YOU WIN!!

Summary****Times have surely changed. Not for the better, the times we live in now make me cringe. I want the best for my offspring and generations to come, but I see with these times we are in that may be impossible to be done. I just wanted to, I NEEDED to talk a little about what's going on in the time I'm living in right now. These next few pieces will speak on it so please pay attention and don't sleep on it.

We Live In A Time When….

We live in a time where it is a tall order for us to ask/pray that our children live longer than we do. We live in a time where it doesn't matter how fancy the school our children/grandchildren go to, we should be happy when they arrive back home. They could go to a private or church-based school, their safety is still not guaranteed. We live in a time where girls/women respond positively to the words bad bitch, and aren't interested in the men/gentlemen who refer to them as a beautiful lady/woman. Our young women think something is wrong with a man that opens doors and pulls out chairs. Skeptical about the man that doesn't try to have sex with them on the first date. "He must be gay" they say as they forever send a rare, good one on his way. We live in a time when it seems everyone is posting videos of everything that is going on around them whether it's good or bad. They prefer holding a camera to offering a helping hand. We live in a time where sick minded people can watch our little girls twerk and bend it over while a little boy's family, neighbor or friend is encouraged to get behind her and do moves that only grown folks should be doing, because some sick ass person is watching, encouraging and recording it. As soon as I notice what kind of video it is, I'm done, I'm not liking, sharing, or giving you views for such garbage. I don't think it is funny nor am I amused in any way. We live in a time when, if a teen gets pregnant it is celebrated with reveal parties, and baby showers giving them and their peers the idea that having a baby so young is the thing to do.

Using babies as accessories when they go out in public and leaving them with you, wherever, with whomever all of the rest of the time. We are living in a time when the lower the guys pants are off of his ass the more girls find him attractive, oh he is the one they think they want to be with. This time we live in also includes the most disrespectful guys having young women trying to be faithful and loyal. She's willing to do anything to make him pay attention to her and only her. No, it never works, but our daughters, nieces, sisters, cousins and friends have no self-esteem and are in need of someone to tell them they are beautiful, smart, or simply validate them. We live in a time when this is what a guy pretends to do to get her, then disrespect her shortly after. She stays because she is always hoping for that one nice past moment they had or something nice he once did in the past, and he is no fool. He will occasionally do something nice every now and then, but be a total asshole all of the rest of the time. The more he beats her the more she thinks he loves her...SMH. We live in a time when people could be married less than a week, be well known for getting pregnant early, or for making a sex tape. People are seeking fame no matter how or what they have to do to get there. A time when T.V. preachers and rappers are living the same type of lives, and it's filmed for us to see. We live in a time when men having several children by several different females is something to get a fist pound over. A female with several fathers for her children gets a high five on the way to the nightclub same days every week to look for her next baby's father. We live in a time when parents are ready to fight a grown up telling their child something to correct or discipline them even though they know that the child is wrong. We live in a time when the age that our children are being arrested and sent away is getting younger and younger, possibly because of that same parent that doesn't want their child disciplined by a teacher, neighbor, not even an aunt/uncle or grandparent. I say to those please keep your seeds away from me, because they're liable to be planted properly when you come back to retrieve them. We are living in a time when it seems people are judging same sex couples, when they seem to be the only ones raising children that are doing positive things, making good grades, getting awards, creating new inventions at young ages. They are usually greatly loved and respected as parents. Their lifestyle usually has no bearing on the type of person, parent, friend, etc. that they are. Usually, the ones that are doing the judging don't know what their own children are doing. We are living in a time when nothing is private, and almost everyone is up to something. We live in a time when knowledge is shunned and boozing and fast living is what is glamorized. It is what ignorant people think should always be done. We live in a time when it's hard to trust anyone, especially the government. Oh, maybe I shouldn't say that. Well, I already did. I know for doing or saying less people have ended up dead. We live in a time when children are killing their parents and grandparents just because they said they can't go hang out with friends. We live in a cold heartless time where someone can kill, harm, hurt an infant and just go about the rest of their day as if nothing happened and show no remorse or empathy about it when they are found out. A sick time when a man can go around raping grandmothers and killing them just for the thrill of it. We live in a time when we are safe nowhere work, school, church, home, I really mean nowhere. We live in a time where people that are supposed to be good are supposed to be looking out for us, priests, preachers, parents, grandparents, teachers, police officers, etc., are the ones doing the harm to us and our families. We live in a time where some minds are sick enough to take advantage of a special needs person without feeling anything. We live in a raw time, a sick time, a time when we don't know who is good and who is bad, a time where I can't give an old lady at the bus stop carrying groceries or a mother in the rain with her baby a ride home for fear that she might be the bad person. No more, nice old grannies, no more innocence in sitting on daddy's lap, no more safety while praying in church, no more leaving babies with grandma, no more treating a female like a lady, no more children sitting around respectfully listening to stories of hope and fairytales from loved ones. This time we live in is very saddening to me. I'm sure I didn't get everything that's going on in the times we live in, but I think I got more than enough things that we should be praying about. I know it's not the happy, joy, sexy, joking writes you are used to, but It was on my mind.

Ho Ho Hmmm????

Ho Ho Hmmm!!!!
It seems that it's the time of year when everyone pretends to be in the caring, loving, spirit*
That must be why so many are depressed and no one notices until they decide to end it*
They sent messages and signals you just didn't take notice, now they're gone you at the funeral throwing a fit*
Why why why this for family and friends is a traumatic hit*
Weighing hearts down like a ton of bricks*

I don't celebrate holidays*
I chose to show love, and caring many days*
I show this in many ways*
Giving really shows how forward life pays*

Repeating in a giving circle helping the community in which one stays*

On the holidays people feel generous sending food, clothes and toys for people in need*
So what wear rags, play with nothing and have wish sandwiches to eat until holiday time next year repeats?*
Would be nice if more people were generous many days of the year, month, week*
All those times of the year when you go blind to what others around you seek*
If it's not a holiday those things seem just right out of their reach*
Changing times and seasons determine when and or if they can eat*
Appreciate bread, but oh so very thankful for meat*
Help to sustain them longer keep them on their feet*
Trying to find steady work not always an easy feat*
How would you want me to act if the one in need was you and not me?*
Some can't get around without assistance, maybe no truck or car*
Call to check if they need to go somewhere

it's not that hard*
Maybe they just need a ride down the street
it's not that far*
If it wasn't for the kindness of strangers some
people would starve*
They noticed you looking at them in the
window before the big turkey you just carved*

It's not the first thing on your mind because
you take for granted the simple things*
Hopping in the car for an errand, groceries, or
simply if your phone rings*
Do you ever wonder about that person
walking as you sit in your car bobbing your
head while you sing*
Have you ever thought about if your places
were switched and you had no money, no
food, no car? Stop to think*
Are you just that heartless? Yeah, that's got to
sting*

They may be working hard to make things
meet with their minimum wage job*
They working hard, no need to clutch your
purses they're not trying to rob*
Sitting at home alone on hard times thinking
there is no help in sight, I know that's not your

prob*
Throwing up their hands for a while you just
have to break down and sob*

Don't hold it or hide it succumbing to
suppression*
Carrying many years of hurt, and oppression*
That will definitely have you in the funk of a
deep depression*
Some acting out in many forms of self-
aggression*
Family is minutes away but they feel alone
sitting at home stressing*
Thinking of loved ones, they lost, no longer
her life over no onward pressing*
I see more family on Social Media than in real
life, that's why I'm thinking and addressing*

You forgot people especially family, you're
busy, you don't have time*
I understand people have to work to live, but
life is more than hustle and grind*
Ironically the people that call or come check
on me are not even genetically mine*
Just simply getting invited out to get what you
need to some could be so sublime*
Call someone up instead of texting, "Hey, how

are you? Do you feel fine?"*
I will do you wonders to be so kind*
May actually make you feel really warm and
good inside*
Just know you can't change people. I don't
suggest anyone sit there, waste tears and cry*
No need for that relax your mind*
I'm just stating some facts and y'all know I
didn't speak any lies*
Chos3nOn3Sp3aks scribe supplied 12/12/2015

Summary**When the New Year rolls
around many of us use that as a time to renew
ourselves, re-evaluate our lives and figure out
what can we change to make us better. This
piece is what was on my mind in a recent year
and I decided it should be shared with my
social media friends. I wanted to work on
being more positive about life in general and
offer encouragement to others that may need
it. I think I have reached my goal to be more
positive. I have work to do, but I'm working
on it:)

Encouragement For Your Soul

It's my time, it's my year*
Get the fear up out of here*

No fear is going to rob my soul*
Fear won't allow some to reach a life goal*

Fear is what most of us have*
Paralyzing to our reach and distancing our
grab*
Not reaching for our dreams just speaking
them, gift of gab*
Not getting where you want make you feel
sick make life seem drab*

It's like a disease making some ill*
Like B.B. King said it's gone that thrill*
Allowing another to use negativity to decrease
your mind power, steal*
Holding you hostage abducting your will*

Your will to dream*
You should just scream*
Set yourself free*
Free fall go forward so you can see*
What your life can really be*
You have to do that for you forget about me*
Stop with the worries of what was said by

them, him, and she*
Especially when they're not even trying to be all there is to be*
Sounds like the army, but this is Chos3n On3 Sp3aks*
Not following their own dreams, but hating on everyone else's. Don't you agree?*
Diminishing others because they are weak*
Speaking truth I'm not trying to preach* There are some including me my words are trying to reach*

Sorry fear I don't need you*
My heart has dreams I must see through* My mind has set goals that I must do*
We all have fears that much is true*
Hovcring, crippling, preventing causing us to hold to that excuse*
A strong wind came and away fear blew*
Looking around now it's clear that there is nothing you can't do*
Standing there clear headed and strong*
We're forging forward moving on*
Sorry fear I got things to do goals to reach, so you can pack your shit and get gone*
It's time now to follow our dreams. Fear has

stopped us for too damn long*
Together reaching our goals never too late, so
what if were grown*
I kicked fear hard as I yelled, "Hey coward go
long!"*
Look for me this year, re-introducing me not
fearful, I'm Strong*

Is fear robbing your soul?*
Shake that off let that go*
Follow your dream. Go get that goal*
Creating resolutions new, as people cheer*
Fear is mocking yelling loudly, "Happy New
Year!!"*

Counting on you to fail again*
New year, new you same shit you said once
you're saying again*
You see that pattern look closely You can't
give in*
Do things differently no letting fear win*

HAPPY NEW YEAR EVERYONE!*
Ignite your fireworks shoot fear with your
gun* Soon we'll all cheer, "We won, we
won!"* I'm cheering you on to your goal "Go

get it friend!" I'm leaving encouragement for your soul. Hopefully I'll see you all at the end*

Summary**** This next piece was written for a friend turned family member that passed away. She was a fun high-spirited person that everyone loved. I just wanted to have the chance to remember her with these heartfelt words.

Ode To A Queen

Ode to a queen
Here's to you Adeline*
When I first met you, I was only a teen*
You were always nice, no never mean*
You knew your way around a closet kept your body fluffy, lean*
Matching your outfits to the polish on your hands and feet *
Your style was on point so fresh and so clean*
When I found out you left us, I thought it was a bad dream*
You were urgently needed called home it seems*
You now have another audience for those

songs you'd sing*
Your beautiful smile dulls the sun's shining
gleam*
Your handsome sons always were always on
your team*
God blessed you with men; four diverse men
doing great things in life*
Men that are not indolent, in life they're hard
working earning a price*
They have seen what they want out of life and
taken their slice*
They are using their visions to create
businesses to keep them eating nice*
Bills paid, a roof over their heads and a place
to lay them down at night*
Men that are following their visions going
after what is good and right*
Men seeking education for higher positions on
the ladder reaching for higher heights*
They love you with all of their might*
You left behind many memories; stories filled
with delight*
Your southern accent and the swift way you
spoke*
Whenever I saw you, we always managed to
get in a chuckle before you would go*

You were always so loving, you always
laughed at my jokes*
The way you said "gal" and that special smile
only you wore*
No one else was quite like you if you weren't
feeling someone, you'd let them know*
Not fake 100% the only way to go*
You were a fabulous person I was blessed to
know*
Your offspring are here future families to
grow*
You will not be forgotten. I know that fa'sho*

I hope this piece is accepted positively,
appreciated*
Your life should not cause sadness you created
life and should be congratulated*
Go "Gal" your life should be celebrated*

Adam, Ronald, Donald and Curtis continue to
push to life's greatest tests*
In this sorrowful time, I know you guys can't
help but feel dejected or depressed*
Your mom has gone where there will no
longer be stress*
You have many memories to hold onto,

caress*
You all know as a mother she gave you her
best*
Go on continue to do things to make her proud
she wouldn't expect any less*

Continue to grow positively in your lives*
You may come to have children, nice families
with beautiful wives*
Surpass all the naysayers whatever you want
continue to strive*
You can come to me for anything you need*
Have no doubt I will happily heed*
If I have it it's yours, I'm not prone to greed*
If negativity approaches you, don't bother
walk away just leave*
No negative egos are you required to feed*
You are strong men of valor chosen to lead*
This is an ode to your mother for you to have
and to read*
You have lived a full life so it seems, my dear
Adeline

I bid you adieu until we meet again*
You were known as mother, wife and fabulous
friend*

The love that is known for you will never
end*

Uniquely you, just one of a kind*
Memories of you forever inscribed in our
minds*

Later for now to you sweet Adeline*
As we all say farewell to a fabulous Queen*

Summary**This next piece speaks from
the point of view of a woman in an argument
gone too far. Things were said that hit below
the belt, (maybe on both parts) things she
knew/thought she did to keep her man happy
were called into question, and her feelings
needed a very unique, whole hearted apology
in which she would cry on his shoulders and
then forgive him............ Maybe...........
Tomorrow.

Happy Wife Happy L....??

Dangerous combination you know this is true*
Battle with your woman. Is this what you

really want to do?*

Wiser men have done it stupid at its best*
They said that unspeakable thing that lands
them in the room used by family or guests*
Don't you ever compare me to your ex*
For any man that's an awful mess*
Remember for me to be like her we'd have to
erase the sex*
Also remember while you were working, she
was probably somewhere bent over behind a
revolving door where she yelled, "NEXT!"*

Before you compare me remember this is
where from the start you said you wanted to
be*
Better watch yourself when you try to come
for me*
I'm Chos3n and no one else can ever be she*

Before you compare me to anyone*
Remember that pedestal you put me on could
get kind of heavy trying to hold up more than
one*
You got to put down the others; their dead
POW POW smoking gun*
Being the woman, I am makes me a hot

commodity, nothing new this hasn't just
begun*
With me you get it all and not just a little or
some*
With me you'll get love, great conversation,
laughter and fun*
You can talk slick if you like, but we both
know I come second to none*

Don't come off slick with me bridle your
tongue control what comes out*
I know I've said my share I admit it no doubt*
You should know when you're hitting to low,
I mean I'm an erotic writer what is this really
about*
I'm still the one that has you floating high and
weak at the same time with only my mouth*
I also know you can't resist what I'm holding
down south*
Yeah, look at it stop drooling don't you love
how she pouts*
She's dried now all your fault from vile words
that you spout*
Sasha could be squirting, it's your fault that
she's not*
You spoke stupid bullshit that got Trouble
kicked out*

You tried to shoot shit at me shots fired,
attack, venom, poison*
Of that I am the baddest; insults, attacks, I
have plenty you know foison*

Hope you felt bigger trying to hurt my
feelings*
Nice job, but you shouldn't forget I'm the
woman with whom you have a lifetime of
dealing*

Either love me or leave me because you can't
do both*
This is not one of my cute, little love notes*
There are choices before you. Chos3 wisely I
hope*
I need an apology no it's not a joke*
Let's see what you bring then Sasha and I can
take a vote*
This piece isn't anything like the others I
wrote*

I'm not upset or mad maybe a little hurt*
Just remember you took it to that level first*
Not trying to open the door for those dudes
filled with thirst*

My love is so big my heart threatens to burst*
It's true that loving someone can sometimes
be a curse*
Disagreements with loved ones are truly the
worst*
Whoa look at me slaying as I'm killing each
verse*

Even with my issues medically speaking*
Nothing any woman can do that I can't never
defeating*
This war with me you shouldn't be seeking*
You compared me to someone that in bed is a
lazy, fat, I don't do that, weakling*
I bring it sexy and that's no lie*
She couldn't measure up no matter how hard
she ever tried*
Chronic suffering and discomfort aside*
There's something addicting about my kind of
pie*
Do you wish to challenge, do you wish to
deny?*
You brought the tear, but you didn't make me
cry*
The ball is in your court so what's up guy?*
You inspired this write while I'm naked and

high* LMAO my my my?*
I hope you're upstairs thinking oh why, oh why?*
Hopefully soon you'll apologize*

Summary**A new age poem about loving/feeling someone from an alternative method such as phone, chat, app, or the internet before meeting them physically. Well, it was new age when I first wrote it over 10 years ago.

Before I Meet You

Before I meet you, I just want to say, I pledge myself to you in every way. Not going anywhere I'm here to stay. Before I meet you, I must accept, that the bitter and the sweet will belong to you and me. Before I meet you, we both know of happiness and smiles, sadness and tears, being in love has hopes and fears. Before I meet you, I want you to know sticking with you like glue is what I will do. I'm always showing/proving, I want to be with you. I am the one you need and soon you shall see I'm nothing like your past so accept and love me for me. Before I meet you, I know you have your moods, your stress, your grief, your strife. I'm here to say it will be alright, to future hubby from future wife Before I meet you, I want you to know I'm on/by your side so when things get rough, I won't run, hide, or say goodbye. Before I meet you, these things I had to let you know because once I meet you, I won't let you go. Before I meet you, I hope that you can be my baby, I'll be your boo, Baby I promise, I Love You! It's all because once before I meet you, becomes after I met you there will be no turning back. Do you feel me??

Summary**I wrote this lovely love poem with the goal in mind to include all of the letters of the alphabet in order and still have the piece make sense. This is truly ABC's Like No Other.

ABC's Like No Other

(A)mazing thing for what was once my (B)ewildered spirit. Your love and special way of (C)aring for me and mine lets me know I did choose right. Your (D)ominance to an extent is sexy, and your confidence assures me that we are (E)verlasting. It was a very special moment in my spirit when you offered your (F)amily to me, as mine is such a sorrow.

(G)od has put us together so no upset can survive. Hell may be your zip code, but heaven is all your (H)eart shows me. (I) love you too much for your story to be false about meeting you before, (previous lifetime) it has to be true I know you love me flaws and all never (J)udging my crazy ass. This makes you a (K)eeper in my book. You're my true soulmate, my generous (L)over. I have made my share of (M)istakes and (N)ever do I want to experience life without you. (O)thers have failed me. I know you're (P)erfect for me. A (Q)uitter I am not. Never going anywhere. You (R)espect my feelings and sacrificed your image to satisfy me on several occasions. A (S)pecial man you have such a loving heart. The way mine beats for you makes me excited about my future. I really just want to love you, (T)he way your heart, mind, body and soul desire. I love how we communicate and work to (U)nderstand each other. (V)ersatility in our relationship keeps things fresh and new. Never needing or (W)anting anyone but each other. I'm idyllic, you're exotic like (X)anadu. I adore you (Y)esterday today and tomorrow. Take my hand and let's fulfill our (Z)est for a wonderful life together.

Summary**The next piece just speaks about my writing itself. It just explains that it's all mine straight from my head to the paper. I've been asked several questions about where my ideas come from. I'm just a creative thinker. I can and have written on many topics from sex to death. I have written nonfiction from a fiction point of view. Writing is art and can be whatever or however you want it to be. I think I've shown that in this book.

Stop Ogling Get Googling

You can Google me, but not the things he can do to me*
I pen descriptive all details not just how he's screwing me*
In this lifetime had my share of men and women ogle me*
Haven't found that many that could keep it real, stay true to me*
If I wrote it, it's nonfiction you best believe*
Published as fiction, push it through with ease*
I click that pen hard for a cum release*

Sometimes standing sometimes I'm on my knees*
Pussy opened wide enjoying the breeze*
Mouth makes that dick disappear with ease*
I try so tell me if you're not pleased*
Catch your breath, inhale, can you speak?*
No bones here I'm thick as thieves*
Kiss me wherever you find a crease*

For those of you that say I'm slick in my mouth*
This isn't caveman days, far from it without a doubt*
You really don't like it when you're on that bullshit and I call you out*
Shock enough to make you say ouch*

I'm like 7up's caffeine levels zero you never had it and you never will*
I do all this talking and back it up shit stays ill*
From that sick shit I say to that sick shit I do*
Don't waste time wondering because all that shit is true*
Rich and Trouble always get me through*

That shit you said about being off topic*

If it's sex then it's sex so dude please drop it*
My pussy is leaking grab a mop I see you
watching*

Do my pictures turn you on?*
Are you horny and alone?*
Toni Braxton sang another sad love song*
Listen while in your jail cell writing poems
Never mind get away please move on*
Your 15 minutes of fame is gone*
Out of my way moving along

Always sending info name and number*
I'm married can't you read or don't you
remember*
Flirty, can't help it Sagittarius I was born in
December*
There are no stories posted not one that I have
stolen or used*
All original work, print the headline spread the
news*
Big words on those pieces, buy the book,
never mind you'll just be confused*

Summary**This piece is really just saying
if I judge someone it will be off of what they

have shown me. Judging a person any other way just gets you deceit and pain. Dishonesty is a chosen action. I can love someone to the moon and back, but I can only react to the person they show me that they are. If someone shows you who they are don't look for anything different simply believe them.

IF

If you lie to me, I'll just assume you don't know what the truth is.
If you hurt me, I won't cry, I'll assume you don't know pain.
If you hate me, I'll know you had to love me first. If you never kiss or hug me, it will be your great loss.
If you don't listen to me, I will assume you can't hear. (Deaf)
If you don't speak, I will assume you can't talk. (mute)
If you don't laugh, I will assume you have no sense of humor.
If you cry, I will not think of you as weak only human.
If you fall, I will help you up.

If you break, I will be with you, to help you mend.
If you plant a seed, I will help it grow.
If the lights go out and I can't see, I will take your hand and let you lead.
If you fall tired, I will cover you and place a pillow beneath your head.
If someone brings harm to me, I will move out of the way as you fill them with lead.
If you lose your mind, I will help you find it Even after a bad argument if someone messes with either of us, we can always count on looking across the room and see one another simultaneously rolling up our sleeves cause we're going to beat their asses together.
Tougher Than Leather, Real Love

Summary**This next piece is a play on the letters P-M-S for Premenstrual Syndrome. Many ladies have moody feelings, feel hornier during that time of the month, are more irritable, we crave certain foods or feel depressed. I decided to write about PMS with a funny creative take on the subject, by capitalizing only the letters P, M and S throughout the entire piece. What is there to

do when you can't have sex the original way.
Get creative and use what resources you have.
Welcome to patches and plugs week.

PMS!!!!

PatcheS and PlugS week*
Sorry you can't watch the PuSSy Skeet*
that'S long for MoSt Men becauSe y'all are
juSt too daMn weak*
if you really want to know yeah, She Still
leakS*
that PuSSy Still throbS She knowS how to
SPeak*
She can't wait till She can let trouble beat*
right now, i'M Sucking that dick, Skilled not
uSing My teeth*
My Mouth iS ready to Swallow your dick*
My Mouth goeS down on it really quick*
not before My tongue takeS a SloPPy lick*
oh, My PuSSy iS jealouS i think*
i feel it She'S going to be Sick*
She'S feenin' So bad for that beautiful dick*

My Mouth iS relaxing Making thingS hollow*
So that whole dick She can Swallow*

in wet, warM goodneSS the dick can juSt
wallow*
Still Soft like a MarShMallow*
but quickly it doeS grow*
hard aS…. hMMM you know????,
that dick waS Solid My Mouth relaxed and
My throat did follow*

well, PatcheS and PlugS for about five to
Seven dayS*
relax and let My Mouth be calgon take you
away*
aS you wait for PuSSy to coMe out and Play*
not fighting a battle but that dick sometiMes
SlayS*
back to My Mouth I won't let nothing waSte*
that dick done took over all My Mouth Spacc*
i'M loving So Much how your juiceS taSte*
My Mouth Speaking that orgaSMic flow*
coMe on baby give it to Me let it go*
you Stroking in My Mouth faSt, but i'M
Sucking you Slow*
Shoving Much dick in My throat*
oh, what a wondrouS Place for you to cuM
that'S fa'Sho*
So, ladieS when you feeling Sexy on that
Monthly flow*

don't forget giving hiM head or a hand job iS
the way to go*
anal workS great alSo, i think you know*
PMS in thiS blog in all capitalS though*
hoPefully i didn't upSet woMen too Much
talking about PuSSy flow*
PMS now i got to go*

Summary**I wrote a piece in 2008 titled
"I'm A Good Person; You Chose Wrong". In
spite of everything I've been through taken
advantage of, used, and abused I still managed
to remain a consistent good woman, I find that
many of those things are still true today in
2021, (I'm more cautious) so I wanted to
distend on the topic from today as well as
yesteryears.

Consistent Good Woman

I make sure my elderly neighbors are well*
Sit and have coffee learn something for a
spell*

I'm the honest friend you seek*
I don't mind your business it doesn't pertain to
me*
My eyes to myself I won't even peek*

If by chance there's something I see*
I shut my mouth, and won't even speak*
You're welcome to my place, but don't lose
my key*

I'll babysit your bad ass kids*
I have so much patience*
Don't take my kindness for weakness*
Goodness gracious*

They'll be sweet with me*
Nope, I'm not above bribery*
They'll know, I'm their favorite auntie*

I'm that woman that is loyal, faithful and
loving to my man*
I'll tell you if yours gets out of line with me,
even if you don't ever speak to me again*
You know in a good friendship I stan*
Your loudest cheerleader your biggest fan*
I'm a person that believes family doesn't
always have to be blood*
They can be Chos3n bond by love*

I believe that without God you have nothing*
God is love, so I'll keep being something*
I'm a person that can be happy for your

success*
Tell you how you slay in that dress*

I'm hurt when you cry*
Forgive you if my patience gets tried*
I'd be hella sad and angry if you died*

I can listen to your issues and secrets*
I know how to be consoling and discreet*
I will definitely tell you have food in your
teeth*

I'll help you if I can because I care about you*
I give honest answers hope you can handle the
truth*

I may post a mean blog or status*
If I don't like the way someone coming at us*

I'm a good person, point blank periodT*
Just don't try to cross me I'm got damn
serious*
Retaliation is brutal, I came to win*
Please don't make me have to tell you again*

Summary**What would happen in my
head if I was called a derogatory word, while

cooking breakfast. Sure, I'll accept certain words while giving him head. I save certain words strictly for the bed. I heard it and it felt out of place. I decided to write about it. Writing is truly fit for any occasion. This did not happen, people it is purely fiction.

You Called Me A What??

How dare you? Are you losing your mind? Called me a bitch when I wasn't giving you head, riding you or licking you down. Even worse I was cooking breakfast in that hot kitchen my nigga please tell me what, was your ass thinking? I probably should ask really what were you drinking? Oh, I scramble those eggs, flip those hotcakes, turn that bacon, it's truly the grits, oh no that oatmeal that will make your skin peel. Yes, I toss the whole pot at your ass. Now you can call me mutha fuka, crazy, silly, fat, lazy, you might even say fuck you, hell even bitch now as I watch that shit slide down your arms and I laugh. I told you before that is the one word that will bring you harm. Now come on get your, trifling, dumb, ignorant, stupid, lazy, lying.... Did I forget one? Oh yeah, your bitch ass in the car so I can take you to the hospital before that knife accidently jumps into your foot. Second or third degree burns I'm thinking you'll think twice about calling me a BITCH again

Summary**This piece is about my marriage of almost 10 years. I had a lot to deal with, but I'm glad I did it. It was accomplished and I made it on my own. I learned from having to do everything, while single parenting with a husband in the home. Going to work and paying some bills is not all a husband is supposed to be. I'm better for doing it now. I have no regrets as I've grown. Written about eleven years ago.

No Regrets I'm Grown

I left the doors open and a hurricane came in. It felt good at first easy, breezy, free so I decided to let things be. Whirlwind romance, a fire roller coaster ride. You promised me you'd stay by my side. I DO'S were said and my life as your wife has now begun. You told me you loved me like you loved no other.

Which is what made me shake my head and shudder. I was open to what you said you wanted house, dog, few kids not a zoo. Tell me why did I lay there in labor suffering alone, no you. Where in the hell were you? GONE I did it alone for not one but two. You were never there, no support of any kind. This just can't keep going on. Going places that require my mate with a sad LQQK on my face. You should be here, never showed up not even late. You knew I had medical issues when we met you said, "No problem I accept". Once again, I sit in the doctor's office alone, no support. LQQKING around the realization that others had someone there really hurt. Alone, grown, and on my own is what's truly going on. I've cried for 10 years you're now my ex. I'm so gone now. I asked who's next? Your loss, your lesson wishing you blessings. Just don't want to wake up one day like a bad sex encounter asking myself, "Damn was that it"?

Summary**This next piece is about Issues I've had after going natural in 2007 when it wasn't a wide spread thing like it is now. I was out there afro and all trailblazing and paving the way. Look at these naturals today acting like they invented it Hell I didn't even invent it. I admire being a naturalista. I'm not sure it's a word, but I'm not deleting it. It's truly nice watching all of the natural afros of all sizes passing by though.

Natural Hair Issues??

I'm wondering if natural hair really is such a bad thing It seems like people just feel like someone should be stoned to death because they don't have a relaxer or any chemical that changes their hair from its natural state. It seems in the African American scene especially, people will accept a weave and a wig before a natural curly, frizzy, nappy style or even locs. I have only experienced negative remarks here on the internet. In real life aside from being touched with or without permission; I have people that are very complimentary about my hairstyle choice from all ethnicities. I think people should work what they have the way they want to. Straight, curly, kinky, wavy, however you dare to wear your hair should be your choice, because the way a person wears their hair doesn't make a person any less nice, loving, intelligent, or just real cool to know. It seems that the problem is usually from other African American Women which I think is just sad. I'm confident in myself and actually love my hair because I know what it took to get here. It would be great if there was more acceptance of the topic.

P.S. I was ahead of my time, in 2021 it's accepted more worldwide. Still some who don't agree, but natural hair will be around long term, wait and see. As I add to this wonderful piece in 2021, I'm beautifully loc'd up. I'm proud of my hair and the journey was a blast. I wouldn't change a thing I learned a lot from my past.

About the Author

Tangela Leopaul Bellard, A 48-year-old author that has been writing poetry and short stories since 1999. She started by posting my pieces to an online writing group years ago. Then eventually developed a fan base through that online writing group. She is a wife, mother, friend and grandmother. Tangela spends her free time writing, sewing, coloring, gardening, singing karaoke, cooking, reading, playing online games and other fun things that provoke laughter or relaxing pleasure. She doesn't do idle time very well. She just like keeping busy. She's never bored, there is always something to do. The author enjoyed writing this book, because it allowed her to play out so many characters from so many different times in her life. The advancement of the authors work can be seen throughout this book. Tangela has stated that she can see how her writing and her style has grown over two decades of writing. Below is how you can get Tangela's previous book and where she can be reached on social media platforms.

https://www.amazon.com/Lick-Over-Tasty-Treat-Lovers-ebook/dp/B074LB6XNG

Email: Chos3nOn3Sp3aks@gmail.com
Chos3nOn3Sp3aks2016@gmail.com
FB: Chos3n_On3_Sp3aks
Twitter Chos3nOn3Sp3aks
https://instagram.com/stories/
IG:

googl3_m3_im_chos3non3sp3aks
IG:
famously_m3_chos3non3sp3aks
Sound Cloud: Chos3nOn3Sp3aks